"Trees have long been a symbol of rebirth, but perhaps nowhere more so than in Hiroshima and Nagasaki. Many not only survived the atomic bombings in 1945, but thrived, giving human survivors hope that they, too, would again be healthy and whole. Hideko Tamura Snider has taken that idea a step further, suggesting to children, with thoughtful illustrations by Mari Kishi, that the trees also give the gift of understanding and healing, lessons a new generation must learn if we are ever to move forward together in peace."

Clifton Truman Daniel
Board Member, Harry S. Truman Presidential Library

When a Peace Tree Blooms

Story by Hideko Tamura Snider
Illustrations by Mari Kishi

All profits from the sale of this book will be donated to charities supporting the children of Fukushima.

For my granddaughter Jordan,

all the children of the world,

and those yet unborn.

On a sunny spring day, Mari and her dog Chip

took a walk into the woods.

Chip romped and played chasing birds.

Mari laughed at his antics.

How beautiful it was!

Soon they saw an old man and a woman in the forest.

What could they be doing?

"What are you doing?" Mari asked the old woman.

The woman opened her hand and there appeared

a tiny little object.

"What is it?"

"It's a very special seed," smiled the old man.

"We're going to plant it here."

"Why?"

"Would you like to hear our story?"

"Yes, of course."

"When we were much younger," began the old man.

"There was a war with a faraway country across the ocean.

It lasted a long time.

Then, the faraway country dropped a scary new bomb

on the town where we both lived.

In an instant, our town burned down.

Many people had burns.

Many people died.

When the war ended, our house was gone.

There was no food to eat, no clothes to put on.

We were wet in the rain.

'What are we going to do?' we asked each other.

We collected scrap wood and built a tiny shack.

Shacks just like ours began to pop up around us.

We did everything we could for many years to stay alive.

Little by little, life began to return to the way it used to be,

with new roads and bridges, schools and shops…

Some of us even built new homes with vegetable gardens.

Our town was slowly coming back to life.

But the new bomb had spread something called radiation.

Some people who had been well became sick from it.

No one knew that radiation could be such a scary thing.

Until then, a small amount was used to cure sick people.

But all this radiation contaminated the woods and the sea.

The animals and the fish also became sick.

Then, one day, a visitor from the faraway country

that dropped the bomb wandered in.

One neighbor who saw him shouted,

'It's your fault that everything got ruined!'

The visitor's expression turned sad.

He looked all alone.

We felt sorry for the man and invited him into our own home.

Serving tea and cakes, we comforted him, telling him,

'The fighting was between the countries, not between us.'

He was very glad to hear it, saying thank you, 'Arigato.'

He took out an old pouch and handed it to us.

Inside the pouch were little round objects.

'What are these?'

'They are seeds.'

After he gave us the seeds, he was gone.

We decided to plant one seed promptly in front of our house.

'What kind of flower will it have?' we wondered.

We watered it every day and cared for it tenderly.

A little seedling came out.

It grew and grew until it became a big tree.

How fast it grew!

In the fall, fruit appeared.

'They look delicious.'

'Shall we try one?'

After a bite, we each exclaimed,

'Wow!'

We remembered the caring feeling we shared with the visitor.

It made us feel good all over.

We shared the fruit with all our neighbors.

Everyone who ate the fruit experienced that same happy

feeling and found themselves at peace with one another.

'This is marvelous.'

'Let's plant some more!'

We even went across the ocean to the faraway country,

sharing our story of befriending a visitor

and the gift he gave in return.

All the people who ate the fruit became joyful,

and they sang and danced together.

They felt happy and peaceful

as they remembered their own caring experiences.

And everyone said,

'This must be a Peace Tree!'

We've been planting the seeds ever since,

to bring peace and happiness around the world."

"But we've grown old,

and this might be our last planting," sighed the old woman.

"Who will plant them after us?" she wondered aloud.

"I WILL!" Mari said with a big smile.

The seeds she and others plant will grow to become tall trees,

bearing many more fruits of peace to share.

Will you join them?

Hideko Tamura Snider was a child in Hiroshima when the city was destroyed by an atom bomb at the end of WWII. She survived with injuries and was ill for some time. Her mother did not survive. A quest for the true meaning of life and humanity began early for Hideko, poignantly chronicled in her book *One Sunny Day*, published in 1996. She lives in southern Oregon, USA. In 2010, she received an honorary doctorate in Humane Letters from the College of Wooster citing her contributions through publications, a lifetime of human services in private and public sectors, and an active speaking schedule addressing issues of "survival, hope and grace in the face of nuclear war."

For more information about Hideko's reconciliation work, see
www.osdinitiatives.com

Mari Kishi was born in Osaka, Japan. A graduate of Kwansei University and Musashino Art School, Kishi worked with editing children's books and educational programing for the NHK, Japan's national broadcasting company, before writing and illustrating for children's stories. Beatrice Potter was her favorite author. She loves to work in warm and soft colors. She lives in Tokyo, Japan, with her architect husband and two daughters. She is a painter in oil and ink brush. Her hobby is practicing Yoga.

Author's Credits and Appreciation

My profound gratitude to Mari Kishi for her artistry and collaboration.
For valued assistance and support, special thanks to: Samantha Alam, Barbara Barasa, Delfino & Cordelia Arellano, Kathy Bates PhD, Christy Brewer, Melissa Brown, Pat Colwell, Patricia Florin, Addie Greene, Leslie Perkins, Marisa Peterson, Ginger Rilling, Liz Robinson, Miko Rose MD & Jordan, Deborah Rothschild, Deedie Runkel, Janet Seim, Michele Swee, Dorothy Vogel, Sharon Schaefer, Brian Voeller, Estelle Voeller, Rev. Kathy Waugh.

Reviews and Reader Comments:

"Hideko's book is simply beautiful.
I'm grateful there are people in the world writing like she does."
Christopher Alftine, MD,
Partner/internist – Medford Medical Clinic, LLP

"The book that Hideko Tamura Snider and Mari Kishi have
produced is the seed of the peace tree that blooms in the story.
That seed first took root in their hearts and grew into a reconciling
love that can redeem the horrors of history. We need to read this
book with our children and grandchildren, so we too can bear the
gift of peace in a world that so desperately needs it."
Herbert Rothschild, PhD
in English Literature, Harvard University, 1966

"What a powerful, always timely and important message to all of us.
We felt the message of hope very strongly."
Del & Cordelia Arellano,
Retired therapist and teacher

"This is a beautiful story, and an important one to be told.
Your choice to tell it as a story within a story makes it personal and immediate, and works, in my opinion."
Leslie Perkins,
Children's librarian

"A heart warming story with beautiful sweet illustrations. I'd like to pass on a reverence for peace for our future myself, in ways possible for me."
Noriko Hansen,
President, Japanese Association of Southern Oregon

"A beautiful, beautiful story!"
Liz Robinson,
Writer/poet

"Thanks so much for writing this beautiful heartfelt story for the world."
Jane Almquist,
Children's bookstore owner

Made in the USA
Monee, IL
06 March 2020